Bunny's Tale

written *by* Kathleen C. Goldstein

illustrated *by* Brenda Murphy

Childsbeing Publishing

P.O. Box 687 Frederick, MD 21705

www.childsbeing.com

Printed in China

Library of Congress Cataloging-in-Publication Data

Goldstein, Kathleen

Bunny's Tale Written by Kathleen Goldstein

Summary: A stuffed toy rabbit tells the story of his journey to reunite

with his beloved owner and friend, a little girl named Rachel.

ISBN 978-0-615-21334-7

[1. Bunny's Tale, fiction]

Bunny's Tale is dedicated to my daughter Rachel,
who inspired me to write this story about an event
that took place during her childhood.

The life of a child is fleeting.
Remember to cherish each moment.

Justin, Rachel, Joshua and Bunny, Easter Mt. Vernon 1989

I would like to thank my husband Jeff for his unfailing support for my project to write and self-publish *Bunny's Tale*. I am indebted to my illustrator Brenda Murphy for bringing the text alive with her beautiful watercolor paintings for *Bunny's Tale*. I want to give my special appreciation to my daughter Rachel Goldstein for her graphic design work on the book. There is a special person that I owe my creative spirit to and that is my beautiful mother, Lillian Kelly Ahlers, who always nurtured my creativity.

It's a lovely spring day here at Maggie's Toy Shoppe and the window where I'm sitting is warm and sunny.

Oh, look! There's a lady peeking in and she's smiling at me! Maybe that lady wants to buy a toy bunny like me. I would really like to belong to someone.

Here comes the lady now. I hope she picks me to go home with her. I like the shop owner, Maggie. She is very nice, but I want to live in a real home and have my very own friend. I feel like I've been sitting and sitting on this shelf for a long, long time.

Look, the lady is talking to Maggie! "Good morning, Maggie," the lady says. "Hello, Mrs. Kelly. How can I help you today?"

Mrs. Kelly tells her, "I would like to buy my little girl a present for Easter. I like the brown bunny that's on the window shelf, the one with the long floppy ears, white fluffy tail, and light blue bow."

Hooray! Mrs. Kelly is going to buy me! I can't believe it! I'm finally going to have a real home and my very own friend!

Maggie says, "Goodbye, Bunny. Have fun in your new home." I'm a little sad to say goodbye to Maggie and my friends at the shop, but I'm very excited to go to my new home!

The sky is so blue, the birds are chirping, and the air smells like lollipops. This must be spring! I see pink flowers on the apple tree and yellow daffodils that look like little bells. Over there by the bush with the little berries, I see a bunny that looks just like me! Sometimes I wish I were a real live bunny, so I could romp around free in the grass and eat lots of lettuce from a garden. Except, if I were a real bunny I probably would not be allowed to live in a house and I certainly would not be allowed to cuddle in bed with my new friend, because real bunnies have to live outside.

Oh, this must be my new home. Mrs. Kelly lays me down on a mound of soft and cuddly grass. I can't wait until tomorrow when I will meet my new friend. But right now I am feeling very sleepy.

I hear the sounds of little giggles coming into the sunlit room. Then a little girl with golden curls gently picks me up and says, "Hello bunny. My name is Rachel and your name will be Bunny. This is my big brother Justin and my little brother Joshua." I like Rachel. She is gentle and nice.

Rachel takes me everywhere with her, except to school. Some days we go to the stores with her mommy. On other days we go outside and play on the swing set. When we are swinging together, Rachel yells out, "Wee! Look Bunny, we can almost touch the sky!"

Today Rachel is at school. No bunnies are allowed at school, except on special show and tell days. Rachel has a lot of friends on her bed. Let's see, there is Riley, her brown-haired doll, and Lexy, her striped cat that purrs when Rachel pushes a little button on her stomach. Then there is Zoey, the brown and black puppy, Sammy, the big white bear with the green bow-tie, and Chance, the chestnut horse.

My favorite time of day is bedtime because this is when Rachel reads to me or tells me a story. Her favorite stories are about horses or cats. Rachel loves horses so much that she says someday she is going to have her own horse and she will jump him over big fences. His name will be Chance, just like the horse that lives on her bed.

Uh-oh! What is happening? Mr. and Mrs. Kelly are wrapping dishes in paper. They are putting towels, lamps, and salt and pepper shakers into a box. I wonder if they are going to put me in a box!

Rachel says, "Don't worry, Bunny, you are not going into a box. You are going on the airplane with me. We are moving from our house in Maryland to a new house in Danville, California."

"Goodbye, house," says Mrs. Kelly.

Wow! We are on the airport bus. Soon I will be on the airplane with Rachel and the whole Kelly family. We are going to fly all the way to San Francisco, California. I wonder if there are bunnies in California.

Rachel, Rachel, you forgot me! Look at me, Rachel! Here in the window! Please, turn around and look at me! I yell and yell for Rachel, but she does not hear me.

I hear the muffled voice of the bus driver as he talks on the phone to someone. The bus driver says, "Yes, yes, I found a little brown bunny with long floppy ears, a cute nose, a little white tail, and a bright blue bow. Okay, I'll put the bunny in a box and mail him to 8 Harmony Lane in Danville, California, 94526."

I miss Rachel and I am a little scared inside this dark box! But I don't mind because soon I will be with Rachel in California.

Someone is opening my box! It must be Rachel. Oh no! This is not Rachel, and it's not Mrs. Kelly either. It is another lady.

"Oh my, what a cute bunny! I will put you on my white chair," the lady exclaims.

The lady never talks to me. She doesn't play with me. She never takes me on rides, and she never, ever tells me stories like Rachel used to do. I miss Rachel with all my heart! I miss her hugging me, reading to me and taking me places. Now all I do is sit and sit on this fancy chair.

"I don't know where Bunny could be. He should have arrived by now. Maybe he's lost!" Rachel sighs.

Mrs. Kelly decided to go to the post office to see if she could find any information on what happened to Bunny. Mrs. Kelly says to the postmaster, "Good morning, Sir. My name is Mrs. Kelly. I am looking for a box that my little girl was expecting four weeks ago. It contained her stuffed bunny. Do you remember if you received a box addressed to Miss Rachel Kelly, 8 Harmony Lane, Danville, California?"

The postman replies, "No, but a box was delivered to 18 Harmony Lane a few weeks ago."

"Oh, dear," Mrs. Kelly says. "I suppose that Bunny was in the box that was sent to 18 Harmony Lane by mistake! Oh, I must go there right away!"

Why, it's Mrs. Kelly! I'm over here! Mrs. Kelly, here in the window! Oh no! Mrs. Kelly doesn't see me! I wonder what Mrs. Kelly is writing.

Dear Owner of
        18 Harmony Lane,

My daughter, Rachel, forgot her brown, stuffed bunny on the airline bus in Maryland a month ago. The bunny has long floppy ears, a cute nose, a fluffy white tail and a blue bow. There is a red and white "Dakin" tag on the bottom of the rabbit. My little girl misses her bunny very much. The postman delivered the bunny to 18 Harmony Lane by mistake. The box was supposed to be delivered to 8 Harmony Lane. If you received a box with a brown bunny inside, please deliver him to our house at 8 Harmony Lane.
                    Thank You,
                    Mrs. Kelly

Oh no, she's leaving! Mrs. Kelly, come back! Please come back! But she cannot hear me.

I'm curious about where the lady is taking me. Perhaps she is taking me back to the post office or perhaps she is going to send me back to Maryland! That would be a disaster because Rachel doesn't live in Maryland anymore; she lives in California!

"Look, Mommy, a box! Maybe Bunny is inside!"

I hear Rachel's voice! The sweetest voice in the whole world!

"Bunny, Bunny! You're finally home! I love you, Bunny, and I missed you so much! I will never EVER lose you again!" Rachel shrieks with excitement.

I missed you too Rachel, and I love you.

History of Names in the Book

The family name Kelly is my mother's maiden name. I always loved her last name, for it is a true link to my Irish ancestry. I also used my niece's first name Margaret (Maggie) for the name of the store where Mrs. Kelly purchases the classic Dakin plush rabbit for Rachel.

Chance, the chestnut horse who lived on Rachel's bed with the rest of her stuffed toys, is named after Rachel's beautiful Oldenburg horse Chance. My husband and I purchased Chance for Rachel in her late teens.

Riley and Lexy, the names of the doll and cat on Rachel's bed, are named after my little cousins.

If you look closely on page 21, you will notice two books lying on the bed; one title is *Shannon is Born in Idaho* and the other is *I Painted You a Rainbow.* These are the titles of my new books that will be available in the near future.

Dakin

I have a bunny that looks real. It got lost one time. Well I was geting off the bus when I remembered my bunny. I forgot at the heatz so I told the bus driver. But he sent it to the wrong house we thougt she was lost forever. One day mom said she had to go some where but she didn't tell us she went to the mail survice and got bunny! I was so hapoy!

Thanksgiving Day, November 1989

Kathleen Goldstein

Kathleen has an English degree from Saint Mary's College in Moraga, California and an early childhood education degree from The State University of Farmingdale, New York. Kathleen finds her inspiration for her children's stories from her own children's childhoods. All three children are now in their twenties. However, their childhood echoes vividly back to the writer who finally has the time to write. Katheen lives in Frederick, Maryland with her husband Jeff and beautiful German shepherd, Zoey.

Brenda Murphy

Brenda is a graduate of Frostburg State College in western Maryland. As a freelance artist and illustrator, her work includes murals, greeting cards, posters and fantasy illustration. Children and nature are constant inspirations for her work. Brenda lives with her husband and two cats in Frederick, Maryland.

In addition to *Bunny's Tale*, Kathleen and Brenda are collaborating on two new books: *Shannon is Born in Idaho* and *I Painted You a Rainbow.*

Visit us at *www.childsbeing.com.*

PRINTED and BOUND in CHINA